FRANZ BRANDENBERG

LEO and BIG I

illustrated by ALIKI

RED FOX

A Red Fox Book

Published by Random House Children's Books
20 Vauxhall Bridge Road, London SW1V 2SA

A division of Random House UK Ltd
London Melbourne Sydney Auckland
Johannesburg and agencies throughout the world

Text © Franz Brandenberg 1982
Illustrations © Aliki Brandenberg 1982

1 3 5 7 9 10 8 6 4 2

First published in the USA by Greenwillow 1982
First published in Great Britain by The Bodley Head 1982
Red Fox edition 1994

Printed in Hong Kong

RANDOM HOUSE UK Limited Reg. No. 954009

ISBN 0 09 929441 9

FOR PAULINE AND ANGELA

CONTENTS

CHAPTER ONE
THE SCARE

"Do you have any bright ideas,
   Leo?" asked Emily.

"Let's scare everybody," said Leo.

"How do we do that?" asked Emily.

"We'll ring people's doorbells,"
   said Leo. "Then we'll run away."

"That won't scare them,"
   said Emily.

"It will make them angry."

"Then let's hide behind a tree,"
said Leo.
"And when someone passes,
we shout 'boo!'"

"That will shock them,"
said Emily.
"It won't scare them."

"Then let's dial the telephone,"
said Leo.
"And when someone answers,
we hang up."
"That's naughty," said Emily,
"not scary."

"Then let's make scary faces
at people," said Leo.
"That will make them laugh,"
said Emily.
"Then let's dress up
as scarecrows," said Leo.
"That's a good idea,"
said Emily.

They went to Leo's house
and dressed up as scarecrows.
Leo's mother got angry
when she saw them.
"Who said you could take
my new hat and Father's good suit?"
she said.
"You are supposed to be scared,
Mother," said Leo.
"You could have asked,"
said his mother. "I don't mind
if you wear my old hat
and Father's work suit."

Leo and Emily changed
into the old hat
and work suit.
Then they went outside.

"Someone could get shocked,"

said the mailman.

"Naughty children!"

said an old lady.

But most people

didn't even notice them.

"No one is scared," said Emily.

"Let's try your house," said Leo.

Emily's mother laughed.

"You are supposed to be scared,
Mother," said Emily.

"Let's go to your grandmother's,"
said Leo.
Emily's grandmother
looked scared.
"Don't be scared,"
said Leo.
"It's just us."
"You spoiled it, Leo!"
said Emily.

Save me from the no-headed monster!

"Let's have a look at ourselves,"
said Leo.

They stood before the mirror.

"Help!" screamed Leo.

He ran out the door.

Emily ran after him.

"What's the matter, Leo?"
she asked.

"I am scared of us,"
said Leo.

"I am glad somebody is,"
said Emily.

CHAPTER TWO

THE GARDEN SHED

"Do you have

any good ideas, Emily?"

asked Leo.

"Come on over to our garden,"

said Emily.

"It's about to rain,"

said Leo. "We'll get wet."

"No, we won't," said Emily.

"We can go into my garden shed."

"You don't have a garden shed,"
said Leo.

"Yes, I do," said Emily.

Leo climbed over
the garden wall.
Emily leaned an old door
against the fence.
"Here is my shed," she said.
They crawled under the door.
"That's a good idea," said Leo.
They sat with their backs
to the garden fence.

It began to rain.

"I love to hear the raindrops
on the roof," said Emily.

"But I don't love to feel them
on my back," said Leo.

"Then let's turn around,"
said Emily.

They sat with their fronts

to the garden fence.

"I don't love to feel the raindrops

on my front either,"

said Leo.

"I know it was my idea!"
said Emily.

"My bottom is all wet,"
said Leo.

"My top is soaking," said Emily.

"I want to go home," said Leo.

"We can't go home all wet,"
said Emily. "Let's go
to our garage."
They ran into Emily's garage.

"How will we get dry?" asked Leo.

"Just watch me!" said Emily.

She took off her shirt.

Then she wiped her head with it.

Leo took off his shirt.

He wiped his head with it.

They took off their shoes.

Then they walked around the garage.

The floor was now covered

with wet footprints.

30

They pressed their fronts
against the back wall.
The back wall was now covered
with wet front prints.
They pressed their backs
against the front wall.
The front wall was now covered
with wet back prints.
They pressed their sides
against the side walls.
The side walls were now covered
with wet side prints.

"We are almost dry," said Emily.

"Almost, but not quite," said Leo.

"My feet are getting wet again."

"So are mine," said Emily.

Water was streaming in
from under the door.

"It's a flood!" said Emily.

33

"Here they are!"

said Emily's father.

"We have been looking
all over for you,"
said Leo's father.

"We were in the garden," said Leo.

"Under the old door," said Emily.

"It was Emily's idea," said Leo.

"I have an idea, too,"
said Leo's father.

"What is it?" asked Leo and Emily.

"A nice hot bath for both of you,"
said Leo's father.

"That's a good idea,"
said Emily's father.

CHAPTER THREE

FLAGS FOR SALE

"I wish we had a flag
for our garden shed,"
said Emily.
"How do we get one?"
asked Leo.
"Don't you ever have any ideas?"
asked Emily.

"I saw an advertisement for flags
in the newspaper," said Leo.
"A hundred cost five pounds."
"We don't need a hundred,"
said Emily. "We need only one."

"We could sell
  the other ninety-nine,"
  said Leo.
"At a profit," said Emily.
"That's a good idea."
"If a hundred cost five pounds,"
  said Leo, "then one costs
  only five pence."
"We can sell them for ten pence,"
  said Emily.
"Then we will make a profit
  of five pence on each flag,"
  said Leo.

"Four pounds and ninety-five pence
 on ninety-nine," said Emily.
"That's a lot of money," said Leo.
"Let's order them," said Emily.
"Do you have any money?" asked Leo.
"No," said Emily.
"Neither do I," said Leo.

"How can we buy them then?"

asked Emily. "This was your idea."

"We could borrow

from our parents," said Leo.

"And pay them back

when we have sold the flags."

"That's a good idea," said Emily.

"I have never heard of a flag
that costs only five pence,"
said Emily's mother.
"That's the wholesale price,"
said Emily.
"All right,
I'll lend you two pounds fifty pence,"
said her mother.

44

"My mother didn't believe
that they cost only five pence,"
said Leo.
"Neither did mine," said Emily.
"But she lent me two pounds fifty,"
said Leo.
"So did mine," said Emily.

IT'S HERE!

A week later

a package arrived in the mail.

"Can I open it, please?"

asked Emily.

"It was my idea," said Leo.

"But half the money was mine,"

said Emily.

"Let's open it together,"

said Leo.

"They are very small flags,"
said Emily.
"And made of paper!"
"What did you expect
for five pence?" asked Leo.

"They are not the kind
  you put on garden sheds,"
  said Emily.
"They are the kind
  you stick on birthday cakes."
"A small flag on the garden shed
  is better than none," said Leo.
"Let's start with the selling,"
  said Emily.

They sold the flags

for ten pence each.

They sold them to friends,

to relatives,

even to strangers.

51

When they were finished selling,

they still had fifty left.

"I think we overbought,"

said Emily.

"We only sold fifty."

"We made five pounds,"

said Leo.

"That's what we owe our parents,"

said Emily.

"We didn't make any profit."

"But we have fifty free flags!"
said Leo.

"What are we going to do
with fifty flags?" asked Emily.

"Fifty flags on the garden shed
are better than one," said Leo.
"We have such good ideas!"
said Emily.

Franz and Aliki Brandenberg are a highly successful husband-and-wife team, writing and illustrating their stories from many of their own childhood experiences and from those of their two children Jason and Alexa, now in their teens.

Leo and Emily first appeared in a book simply entitled *Leo and Emily*, also published by Red Fox, and Franz and Aliki have collaborated on this second book featuring the same lovable characters in more enterprising adventures.